W9-BMV-976

# Hey Diddle Diddle

**and Other Best-loved Rhymes**

# Hey Diddle Diddle

### and Other Best-loved Rhymes

Capella

This edition published in 2008 by Arcturus Publishing Limited
26/27 Bickels Yard, 151 - 153 Bermondsey Street,
London SE1 3HA

Copyright © 2008 Arcturus Publishing Limited

All rights reserved. No part of this publication may be reproduced,
stored in a retrieval system, or transmitted, in any form or by any
means, electronic, mechanical, photocopying, recording or otherwise,
without written permission in accordance with the provisions of the
Copyright Act 1956 (as amended). Any person or persons who do
any unauthorised act in relation to this publication may be liable to
criminal prosecution and civil claims for damages.

ISBN: 978-1-84837-140-8

Printed in China

Illustration by Ulkutay & Co Ltd
Compiler: Paige Weber

# CONTENTS

# Hey, Diddle, Diddle

Hey, diddle, diddle,
The cat and the fiddle,
The cow jumped over the moon.

The little dog laughed,
To see such a sport,
And the dish ran away with the spoon.

# Old King Cole

Old King Cole was a merry old soul,
And a merry old soul was he.
He called for his pipe, and he called for his bowl,
And he called for his fiddlers three.
Every fiddler, he had a fine fiddle,

And a very fine fiddle had he.
Twee-tweedle-dee, tweedle-dee, went the fiddlers,
Tweedle-dum-dee, dum-dee-deedle-dee!
Oh, there's none so rare as can compare,
With King Cole and his fiddlers three!

# Pussy-Cat, Pussy-Cat

Pussy-cat, pussy-cat,
Where have you been?
I've been to London,
To visit the Queen.

Pussy-cat, pussy-cat,
What did you there?
I frightened a little mouse
Under her chair.

# It's Raining, It's Pouring

It's raining, it's pouring,
The old man is snoring.
He went to bed,
And bumped his head,
And couldn't get up in the morning.

# Hush, Little Baby

Hush, little baby, don't say a word,
Papa's going to buy you a mockingbird.

And if that mockingbird won't sing,
Papa's going to buy you a diamond ring.

And if that diamond ring turns brass,
Papa's going to buy you a looking glass.

And if that looking glass gets broke,
Papa's going to buy you a billy goat.

And if that billy goat won't pull,
Papa's going to buy you a cart and bull.

And if that cart and bull turn over,
Papa's going to buy you a dog named Rover.

And if that dog named Rover won't bark,
Papa's going to buy you a horse and cart.

And if that horse and cart fall down,
You'll still be the sweetest little baby in town.

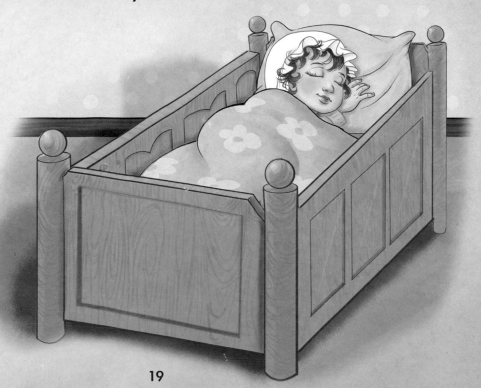

# Ding, Dong, Bell

Ding, dong, bell,
Kitty's in the well!
Who put her in?
Little Tommy Lin.
Who pulled her out?
Little Johnny Stout.

What a naughty boy was that
To try to drown poor kitty-cat.
Who never did him any harm,
But killed all the mice in his father's barn!

# One, Two, Buckle My Shoe

One, two,
Buckle my shoe;
Three, four,
Knock at the door;

Five, six,
Pick up sticks;
Seven, eight,
Lay them straight;

Nine, ten,
A good, fat hen;
Eleven, twelve,
Dig and delve;

Thirteen, fourteen,
Maids a-courting;
Fifteen, sixteen,
Maids in the kitchen;

Seventeen, eighteen,
Maids a-waiting;
Nineteen, twenty,
My plate's empty!

# Pat-a-Cake

Pat-a-cake, pat-a-cake, baker's man,
Bake me a cake as fast as you can.
Roll it and pat it and mark it with B,
And put it in the oven for baby and me.

# Jack Sprat

Jack Sprat could eat no fat,
His wife could eat no lean.
And so, between them both, you see,
They licked the platter clean.

Jack ate all the lean,
Joan ate all the fat.
The bone they picked it clean,
Then gave it to the cat.

# Star Light, Star Bright

Star light, star bright,
The first star I see tonight.
I wish I may I wish I might,
Have the wish I wish tonight.